Little Bear's Picture

BY ELSE HOLMELUND MINARIK

ILLUSTRATED BY DAVID T. WENZEL

HarperFestival®

A Division of HarperCollins*Publishers*

"What are you looking for?"

asked Little Bear.

"I'm looking for my camera,"

Mother Bear called over her shoulder.

"And here it is."

Mother Bear pulled a stack of
books out of the closet.
"Look at all these pictures!" she said.
The books were full of photographs of
Little Bear and Mother Bear and
Father Bear.

Little Bear held up a picture of a
very small bear.
"This bear is so little. Who is it?"
he asked.

Mother Bear laughed.

"Why, that's a sweet little bear that
I knew long ago," she said.

"But who is it?" asked Little Bear.

Mother Bear looked lovingly at the picture.

She gave Little Bear a kiss, and said,

"He was a tiny little bear then.

Now he is bigger, but just as sweet."

"Do I know him?" asked Little Bear.

"Oh, yes, you do," said Mother Bear.

"You know him very well!"

Just then, Little Bear's friends came

to the door.

"Come in," called Mother Bear.

Hen, Duck, Owl, and Cat came in.

Little Bear said, "Look at this!"

11

Everyone came to see the picture.

"Mother Bear says this is a sweet
little bear," said Little Bear.
"And she says that I know him.
Who is it?"

"Hmmm," said Owl.

"Could be—" said Cat.

"He looks familiar," said Hen.

"He is cute!" exclaimed Duck.

"Can't you tell who it is?" asked
Mother Bear.

Cat said, "We don't know any
bears that little."

Owl added, "We only know our
Little Bear."

Little Bear opened his eyes wide.

"That's *me*, isn't it?"

Mother Bear laughed.

"Yes, Little Bear.

That's you, when you were small.

Now you are so much bigger.

Let's take a new picture."

Mother Bear said, "Little Bear,
you stand behind Owl, Cat, Hen,
and Duck."

With a little gentle rearranging,

everyone got into place.

They were ready.

Mother Bear fussed with the camera.

Everyone waited.

Mother Bear looked up.

"No squirming!" she said.

Hen began to wriggle.

"My feathers itch!" she said.

"So do mine," said Duck.

"And my fur—" began Cat.

"Be still!" said Owl.

"Cat!" cried Little Bear.

"Can't you keep your tail still?"

Owl said, "We have to take this

picture before Little Bear grows

any bigger."

Little Bear ran to Mother Bear,

scattering his friends.

"Mother Bear," he cried.

"I'm not growing bigger, am I?"

Mother Bear put down her camera.

She hugged Little Bear.

"Growing bigger takes time—

lots of time.

So let's all get back in place."

Owl said, "Little Bear, you were

littler in that picture."

Hen added, "And now you are big."

Duck asked, "Can we call you

Big Bear now?"

"No!" Little Bear shouted.

"I'm Little Bear, and I like it that way!"

Mother Bear said, "Not to worry—

when you grow bigger you'll like it, too."

"Back in place, everybody,"
said Mother Bear.
"Look happy!"
Snap! The picture was taken.

"Good!" said Mother Bear.
"And now I will take a picture
of Little Bear all by himself."
Everyone else stepped aside.

"Stand by the chair," said Mother Bear.

"That way we can tell if you're growing."

Little Bear stood tall and said,

"The chair can't grow, but I can!"

Snap! Mother Bear took the picture.

"Playtime, everybody!" said Mother Bear.

Little Bear turned a somersault.

Cat rolled on his back.

Hen, Duck, and Owl flapped their wings.

"Mother Bear," asked Little Bear,
"when will the pictures be ready?
When can I see them?"
"It takes a little time," said Mother
Bear, "but you'll see them soon."

Little Bear worried, "But if it takes too long, I'll have grown already.

Will I see them before I am a big bear?"

"You'll see them long before you are
a big bear," said Mother Bear.
"And besides, you can grow and
grow as much as you like.
You will always be my Little Bear!"